A Wish to be a Christmas Tree

By Colleen Monroe

Illustrated by Michael Glenn Monroe

Sleeping Bear Press

Sleeping Bear Press™

315 E. Eisenhower Parkway, Ste. 200
Ann Arbor, MI 48108
www.sleepingbearpress.com

Sleeping Bear Press is an imprint of Gale, a part of Cengage Learning.

20 19 18 17 16 15

Library of Congress Cataloging-in-Publication Data

Monroe, Colleen.
A wish to be a Christmas tree / author, Colleen Monroe; illustrator,
Michael G. Monroe.
    p. cm.
Summary: Feeling sad because no one chooses it as a Christmas tree, a
bedraggled forest pine discovers the importance of being appreciated all
year long.
 ISBN 978-1-58536-002-4
[1. Pine—Fiction. 2. Christmas trees—Fiction. 3. Animals—Fiction. 4.
Stories in rhyme.] I. Monroe, Michael (Michael G.), ill. II. Title.
PZ8.3.M758 Iaan 2000
[E]—dc21   00-009985

Printed by China Translation & Printing Services Limited, Guangdong Province,
China. 15th printing. 07/2010

To Matthew and Natalie, our precious two,

Mom and Dad wrote this book for you.

To Mom and Dad Tokai, thank you for your love and support.

Every year as traditions go,
they get in their cars at the first sign of snow,
and head to the farm at the edge of town,
to cut the family Christmas tree down.

As Christmas neared, the trees rejoiced,
for families would come and make their choice.
Which trees would go and which would stay,
"Oh, please pick me," the trees would say.

"Take me to your home!" said the fat Scotch pine.
"Dress me with bulbs and lights!" said the fir so fine.
They all were excited except for one,
he knew that his days of being picked were done.

"I've seen my sisters and brothers, daughters and sons,
grandkids and great grandkids picked, one by one.
I'll never be taken home, I'm too big and too tall."
His sobbing and crying made his pine needles fall.

A little squirrel was wandering by
and stopped to hear the big tree cry.
"Take heart my friend and don't you fear,
to many of us you are so dear."

"Your branches keep us safe and warm,
you are our shelter from the storm."
A cardinal flying by chirped in,
"You are my safety from the wind."

Said a white-tail deer who was walking through,
"Cheer up big friend because I need you.
Your needles give me a nice soft bed,
a place to lie down and rest my head."

"These things you say to me are kind,
but nothing can really change my mind.
All my life I've wanted to be,
someone's special Christmas tree."

With that he drew his branches in,
and closed his eyes to dream again,
and wish that someday he would be
more than just a great, big tree.

Fast asleep in dreams far away,
he did not hear the little squirrel say,
"You will be our Christmas tree,
let us decorate you for all to see."

"Come gather around," the little squirrel cried,
to woodland animals both far and wide.
"We need to act without delay,
to end our great big friend's dismay."

"He is our friend, this wonderful tree,
and do you know where we would be
without the special things he gives?
I don't know how we all would live!"

"Without ever complaining he's given these things,
yet never knowing the joy that he brings.
Offering friendship from the very start,
never once revealing the dream in his heart."

"Everyone should bring a treasure,
so our giant friend can measure,
the love for him that our hearts hold,
the feelings that we've never told."

Each animal came with gifts to bear,
over ground, through the trees, and some through the air.
With acorns, icicles, and berries so bright,
they worked and trimmed into the night.

The crows searched their nests full of shiny things,
hoping to find the perfect present to bring.
There among their treasures found from afar,
was the most beautiful, bright, shining star.

His woodland friends decorated him
with special things hanging from every limb.
Acorns were dangling off branches strong,
berries were strung as a garland so long.

The first morning sun brought a wondrous sight,
as icicles glimmered and captured the light.
Colorful birds perched all over the pine,
as beautiful as bulbs and just as fine.

Blue jays as blue as a crisp winter day,
cardinals bright red perched near doves soft and gray.
The birds were singing so soft and clear,
their most beautiful songs for the pine tree to hear.

The big tree stirred and opened his eyes,
and what he saw was such a surprise.
"You have made me beautiful for all to see,
and now I am a Christmas tree."

"You are more than just a Christmas tree,"
they said to him, "Why can't you see?
You are special to us every day of the year,
we would be sad if you weren't always near."

"We're glad you stayed with us all these years,
but we're sorry that it caused you tears.
We should have told you the many ways
you are special to us and brighten our days.
Through winter and spring, summer and fall,
you are always here to help us all."

With that they gathered around the tree
and suddenly the tree could see,
it wasn't as important to be a Christmas tree,
but to always be the best friend you could be.

And every year to celebrate
they come together on that date,
to decorate from end to end,
the special tree that is their friend.

Since a very young age MICHAEL GLENN MONROE has known that he has wanted to be an artist. A self-taught painter, he spends much time meticulously honing his craft, often teaching himself new and unique techniques to add to his paintings. His realistic wildlife paintings have garnered him many honors throughout the years.

COLLEEN MONROE lives in Brighton with her husband, Michael and their twins, Matthew and Natalie. She is a graduate of the University of Michigan and worked in advertising for several years prior to writing *A Wish to be a Christmas Tree.*

As in life, Michael's illustrations are the perfect match to Colleen's charming verse. *A Wish to be a Christmas Tree* is Michael's third book with Sleeping Bear Press and Colleen's first. Michael released *Buzzy the bumblebee* and *M is for Mitten: A Michigan Alphabet* in the fall of 1999 and is the illustrator for the forthcoming *S is for Sunshine: A Florida Alphabet.*